Baer, Gene,
1927-

Thump, thump, rat-a-
tat-tat.

$13.80

Baer, Gene,
1927-

Thump, thump,
rat-a-tat-tat.

$13.80

DATE | BORROWER'S NAME

THUMP, THUMP,
Rat-a-Tat-Tat

by Gene Baer

Illustrated by Lois Ehlert

A Charlotte Zolotow Book

HarperCollins*Publishers*®

To Kara, Alyssa,
and Christian—G.B.

Special thanks
to band member
Jim Dinsch—L.E.

Thump, Thump, Rat-a-Tat-Tat
Text copyright © 1989 by Gene Baer
Illustrations copyright © 1989 by Lois Ehlert
Printed in Hong Kong.
Library of Congress Cataloging-in-Publication Data
Baer, Gene, 1927–
    Thump, thump, rat-a-tat-tat

    "A Charlotte Zolotow book."
    Summary: A distant marching band grows larger and
louder as it nears, and then softer and smaller as it
goes away again.
    [1. Bands (Music)—Fiction.   2. Sound—Fiction]
I. Ehlert, Lois, ill.   II. Title.
PZ7.B13894Th 1989   [E]   88-28469
ISBN 0-06-020361-7
ISBN 0-06-020362-5 (lib. bdg.)
ISBN 0-06-443265-3 (pbk.)

Rat-a-tat-tat
Rat-a-tat-tat
THUMP, THUMP
THUMP, THUMP

Distant drums
Chirping horns
Rat-a-tat-tat
Rat-a-tat-tat

Big as ants
Loud as crickets
THUMP, THUMP
THUMP, THUMP

Pounding drums
Squawking horns
Rat-a-tat-tat
Rat-a-tat-tat

Big as crickets
Loud as birds
THUMP, THUMP
THUMP, THUMP

Piping flutes
Purring drums
Rat-a-tat-tat
Rat-a-tat-tat

Big as birds
Loud as lions
THUMP, THUMP
THUMP, THUMP

Festive colors
Flashing brass
Rat-a-tat-tat
Rat-a-tat-tat

Thunder coming
Getting louder
THUMP, THUMP
THUMP, THUMP

side drum

flute

bass drum

trombone

tuba

Marching band
All in tune
Rat-a-tat-tat
Rat-a-tat-tat

trumpet

Thunder passing
Getting softer
THUMP, THUMP
THUMP, THUMP

Festive colors
Flashing brass
Rat-a-tat-tat
Rat-a-tat-tat

Small as birds
Soft as lions
THUMP, THUMP
THUMP, THUMP

Piping flutes
Purring drums
Rat-a-tat-tat
Rat-a-tat-tat

Small as crickets
Soft as birds
THUMP, THUMP
THUMP, THUMP

Pounding drums
Squawking horns
Rat-a-tat-tat
Rat-a-tat-tat

Small as ants
Soft as crickets
THUMP, THUMP
THUMP, THUMP

Distant drums
Chirping horns

Rat-a-tat-tat

Rat-a-tat-tat

THUMP, THUMP

THUMP, THUMP

flags

brass instruments

woodwind instrument

percussion instruments

flute

trumpet

trombone

tuba

side drum

bass drum